A Deadly
Tonic

Eliza Thomson Investigates

Book 1

By

VL McBeath

P9-AGT-723

A Deadly Tonic
By VL McBeath

Copyright © 2019 by VL McBeath, Valyn Publishing
(a trading company of Valyn Ltd).

For more about this author please visit:
https://vlmcbeath.com

All rights reserved. No part of this publication may be reproduced, distributed,
or transmitted in any form or by any means, including photocopying, recording,
or other electronic or mechanical methods, without the prior written
permission of the publisher, except in the case of brief quotations embodied in
critical reviews and certain other noncommercial uses permitted by copyright
law. For permission requests, write to the author at:

https://vlmcbeath.com/contact/

*

Editing services provided by Susan Cunningham
(www.perfectproseservices.com)
Cover design by Michelle Abrahall (www.michelleabrahall.com)

ISBNs:
978-1-9999426-4-9 (Kindle Edition)
978-1-9999426-6-3 (Paperback)

Main category - FICTION / Historical Mysteries
Other category - FICTION / Crime & Mystery

First Edition

CHAPTER ONE

A broad smile crossed Eliza Thomson's lips as she peered through the drawing room window into the street below. The lamplighters were nowhere to be seen, but the paperboy was here already. Reading the newspaper with her afternoon cup of tea was her favourite time of the day but today she wouldn't have much time to herself. Those extra twenty minutes would make all the difference.

She hurried down the stairs to the hallway and retrieved the paper from the letterbox before glancing at the front page. More news about the Boer War. She shook her head. Why had they needed a second war? They should have sorted it out first time around. She hurried back up the stairs and settled into her favourite leather armchair before scanning the newspaper for details of the Battersea murder. Surely the police must have worked out by now that someone had poisoned the victim.

She was so engrossed in her search she didn't notice the door open and her husband Archie walk in.

"You're not reading about murders again, are you?"

Eliza glanced up and smiled at the muscular figure of her husband with his greying hair and moustache. "What are you doing home so early?"

"Dr Shaw said I could finish early, and I wasn't going to argue." Archie's soft Scottish accent filled the room as he nodded at the newspaper. "What is it now?"

Eliza sighed. "The Battersea murder. I wrote to the inspector leading the case a couple of weeks ago suggesting the death was the result of poisoning but so far it hasn't been reported. They say they're still looking for the murder weapon." She shook her head. "They've no chance of finding it."

"I really wish you wouldn't get involved in this sort of thing. It's very unladylike."

Eliza frowned at her husband. "I don't care. Since Henry went up to Cambridge I need something to keep me occupied of an afternoon and playing lawn tennis isn't an option."

"Just because we've moved to the city doesn't mean you can't still play."

"It's got nothing to do with the location. In case you hadn't noticed, I'm not as young as I used to be. My joints won't take it any more."

Archie stepped forward and kissed her head. "Well you still look young to me."

Eliza grinned as she gave him a sideways glance. "Only because you're older than me."

"Not by much!" Archie scowled at her before the corners of his mouth turned up. "I can see I'm not going to win here, but isn't there anything else you could do?"

"Such as? I didn't get a degree in science just to sit here

embroidering. Besides, the police are glad of my help. They've written and thanked me about other cases."

"I'm sure they're only being polite."

"No, they're not. Now, what about you? Didn't you have patients to see?"

Archie perched on the chair opposite his wife. "No, unusually we did the ward round straight after dinner and Dr Shaw said he'd take care of anything else that came up."

"That's not like him; it's usually you who does all the work. He must be after something, you watch, he'll want the favour returned next week."

Archie shook his head. "He's not all bad you know. He often helps me out if I've got things I need to do. He was just busy and knew he'd be at the hospital for a few more hours yet."

Eliza folded up the newspaper and placed it on the table beside her. "Well, I'm glad to hear it. Now you're here I'll pop downstairs and ask Mrs Ellis to put an extra cup on the tray for afternoon tea."

"Afternoon tea? I didn't think you bothered when you were by yourself."

Eliza rolled her eyes. "I don't bother with the cakes when I'm on my own but have you forgotten Connie's coming to stay? I've not seen her for months. She should have been here by now, but she sent a telegram this morning to say she'd been delayed."

Archie shook his head. "Of course, I'd completely forgotten. I was going to ask if you'd like to go to the theatre this evening but I don't suppose you'll have time with the catching up you'll want to do. It's nearly four o'clock already."

Eliza smirked at him. "We're not that bad and despite the

late hour, I'm sure Connie would love to go to the theatre, she's not been for years. Besides, she's here for the week and so we've plenty of time to catch up."

"All right then, I'll arrange some tickets. I won't trouble you about afternoon tea though, you'll need at least an hour together before you can be disturbed." He grinned at his wife before he headed back to the door. "Be ready for half past six."

As soon as the door closed behind him, Eliza retrieved the newspaper and picked up where she left off. There it was. The story she was looking for. *The Battersea Murder.* Her eyes sparkled as she read the headline. *Police yesterday confirmed that following a tip-off from a member of the public, they have established that the cause of death in this tragic case was poison.*

"Hurrah!" Eliza giggled as her cheer echoed around the room. She didn't care; it meant that they'd got her letter and would hopefully now be looking for the right person. How the coroner had missed it when she'd clearly noticed it by reading the police reports, she couldn't fathom. She scanned the column quickly before returning to the top to read it properly. They'd given no details of the poison used. Perhaps they didn't want anyone copying the murder; it would be easy enough to do.

As she approached the end of the article, the front doorbell rang. Mrs Ellis would of course answer it but she needed to be in the hallway. It was months since Connie had last been to London and she was keen to hear why she'd been delayed.

The short train of Eliza's beige skirt floated behind her on the stairs as she hurried to the door. "Connie, dear! Come on in, I'm so glad you got here before it went dark. How on earth are you?"

Connie's pale blue eyes sparkled as she grinned at her friend. "All the better for seeing you."

Mrs Ellis stood to one side as Eliza embraced her friend.

"Mrs Ellis, this is my good friend Mrs Appleton. Would you take her cloak and bag to her room while we go to the drawing room? We'll take afternoon tea when you're ready."

"Very good, madam." With a nod, Mrs Ellis left and Connie glanced around the hallway.

"What a fabulous house. You must give me a tour ... after a cup of tea, of course. It looks like you have too many stairs for someone who's just arrived."

Eliza laughed. "You'll get used to it, but perhaps we'll only go up one flight for now. The drawing room's on the first floor."

"My goodness, what a lovely room," Connie said as they entered a large rectangular room sporting two impressive Georgian windows that faced out over the street. She did a twirl between two settees straddling the fireplace. "I think my whole house would fit in here."

"Not quite, although maybe it would if we opened the doors to the dining room." With a grin on her face, Eliza nodded to the double doors at the far end of the room.

"A separate dining room. I do miss that, being in my little cottage." Connie popped her head through the doors before wandering back to the windows. "It's a marvellous street as well. I thought you were mad when you said you were moving, but I can see why you did. Dr Thomson must be doing well at the hospital."

Eliza rolled her eyes. "Well enough, but when Father

heard he'd got the job and needed to move closer to the hospital it horrified him. We couldn't afford anything like this and so Father insisted on giving me some money as part payment for the house. Only on condition that my name was added to the deeds as well as Archie's though. He said if he couldn't spoil me, who could he spoil."

Connie's eyes misted over. "That's kind of him. I bet he misses you."

"I suppose he does, but he never says anything. We visit him most weeks and he keeps himself busy." Eliza raised an eyebrow at Connie. "Is something wrong?"

Connie paused and glanced out of the window at the tree-lined street. "Nothing really, only that your old house in Moreton-on-Thames has been sold."

Eliza's face straightened. "To anyone we know?"

"No, we think it's someone moving down from London but nobody's seen them."

Eliza straightened her back and took a deep breath. "I don't suppose it matters any more. Anyway, enough of that; come and sit with me and tell me why you're so late. Did you miss this morning's train?"

"Well, I suppose I did, but there was a reason for it. You remember old Dr Jacobs from the surgery next door to me? I like to keep an eye out for him and so I called around this morning to remind him I'd be away for a few days and you'll never guess what. He'd only gone and died in his sleep."

"No!"

"Yes! Not that I knew at the time, of course. I knocked on the door and thought it was strange when I didn't get an answer. That was at eight o'clock and by the time his patients started arriving half an hour later, I was worried. In the end, I hurried to the police station and that nice Sergeant Cooper came back to the surgery with me. He ended up breaking the door open. He wouldn't let me go in with him, of course, but a couple of minutes later he came back to the front path to tell us the news."

"How awful for you, it must have been a shock."

Connie put a hand over her heart. "Oh it was, but Sergeant Cooper was ever so good. He told all the patients they'd have to go to Over Moreton if their need was urgent and then he walked me home and made us both a cup of tea. He stayed with me for over half an hour."

A twinkle returned to Eliza's eyes. "That was good of him."

"It was, he had so many other things he needed to do, but he could see I was shaking. I'd only spoken to Dr Jacobs yesterday afternoon, and now, here he was, dead." Connie failed to acknowledge the delight in her friend's face.

"Well, you're here now and I'm very glad you are."

As she spoke, Mrs Ellis knocked on the door and walked in carrying a tray laden with sandwiches, cakes and a large silver teapot.

"I made enough for Dr Thomson in case he comes back," she said, placing the tray on the table. "Will that be all?"

"Yes, thank you, Mrs Ellis. Did Dr Thomson tell you we'll be going out tonight and so won't want to eat until we return home?"

"He mentioned it." Mrs Ellis didn't pause before turning to leave the room.

"Oh dear, I get the feeling she's not happy about that. I suppose we should have given her more notice although we only decided ourselves about half an hour ago."

Her morning trauma apparently forgotten, Connie bounced on the settee like an excited child. "Where are we going?"

"The theatre, although I'm not sure what we're going to watch. Archie finished work early and so he thought it would be a treat. I hope you don't mind."

"Of course I don't mind, as long as it doesn't involve murder. I've had enough of death for one day."

CHAPTER TWO

The following morning Eliza sat up in bed sipping the cup of tea Mrs Ellis had delivered not ten minutes earlier. The room was bright now Mrs Ellis had drawn the heavy velvet curtains back from the windows, but at this time of day she wished she had the guest bedroom on the floor above. Connie would currently be enjoying the morning sun as it streamed through the window overlooking the back garden. Not to worry, this room was bigger and breakfast would be ready in twenty minutes. Being at the back of the house the dining room would be bathed in sunlight as well.

Archie was already seated at the dining table when she arrived.

"You were up early," Eliza said. "Couldn't you sleep?"

"I've one or two things on my mind so I want to be in work early. Mrs Ellis will be here with the tea and toast in a minute."

"I'll go and check on Connie then, she won't want to be late."

Before Eliza stood up, Connie followed Mrs Ellis and her large tray into the room.

"I'm not late, am I?"

"No, not at all. Archie was early, that's all. Did you sleep well?"

Connie smiled. "I did. It's a lovely room and so comfortable. I don't suppose you'll want to move again now you've found this place."

Archie grinned as he reached for the toast. "We're not going anywhere, even if I leave the Brompton. We're central enough that I can walk or take the train to most parts of London. Eliza will have to show you around the neighbourhood. It's really rather nice."

"I don't doubt it." Connie collected some toast and waited for Archie to finish with the butter.

"Thank you for the trip to the theatre last night, it was a wonderful production. I'm glad that evil Mr Gilfain was found out in the end. What a horrible thing to do to poor Dolores. She didn't deserve to have the family business taken from her in such a deceitful way."

"Don't worry yourself about it," Archie said. "It was only a musical, things like that don't happen in real life."

"Don't you be fooled," Eliza said. "You read about con men all the time in the newspaper, trying to trick people out of their money or possessions."

Archie rolled his eyes at Connie as he passed her the butter. "Not the newspaper again. If you believe everything in there, you'd think the world had gone to wrack and ruin. It's really not that bad."

Eliza cast him a sideways glance. "Just because you can't see what's happening beyond the walls of the hospital doesn't mean London's a safe place."

"I see enough inside the hospital, thank you very much. Can you pass the jam?"

Eliza scowled as she reached across the table. "What time do you expect to be home tonight?"

"Late, I would imagine. After the treat of a short day yesterday, I'm sure Dr Shaw will have plenty of things for me to do." He stood up and pushed his chair under the table. "I'd better be going. See you later."

Archie hadn't reached the dining room door when there was a ring on the doorbell.

"Who on earth's calling at this time of day? Don't worry yourselves. I'll send whoever it is away." Archie hurried from the room but seconds later they heard a shriek from Mrs Ellis and Eliza and Connie rushed to the top of the stairs.

"What's the matter?" Eliza leaned over the bannister to see Archie approaching the bottom of the stairs and a man lying prostrate in the hall.

"H-he ... he lunged at me and fell through the door." Mrs Ellis's voice trembled as Archie knelt beside the man. "He looked deranged ... his eyes..."

"Thank you, Mrs Ellis," Archie said. "Why don't you go back to the kitchen, I'll take care of this."

Mrs Ellis didn't need telling twice and had disappeared by the time Eliza reached the bottom of the stairs. "Who is he?" She bent down to pick up the man's bowler hat, which had fallen to the floor.

"White," the man spluttered as he grabbed hold of Archie to pull himself up. "Reginald White. A-are you a doctor?"

"Yes, I am." Instinctively, Archie put a hand across the man's fevered forehead before feeling for his pulse.

"You've got to help." The man's eyes were wild. "They're trying to kill me."

"Who are?" Eliza was on her knees beside him.

"My..." His head fell forward and he slumped back to the floor.

"Your what...?"

"We haven't time for that," Archie said. "He needs urgent medical attention. His pulse is racing but very weak. Can you stay here and make him comfortable while I go to the hospital and get them to send a carriage?"

"I'll go and see how Mrs Ellis is," Connie said. "She looked rather shaken."

Eliza turned around as Connie backed away towards the stairs leading down to the kitchen.

"Ask her to make you both a cup of extra sweet tea," Eliza said. "You look as if you could do with one too."

"Will you be all right here?" Archie stood up and reached for his hat and coat. "I'll be as quick as I can."

"Yes, but you'd better hurry." Eliza turned back to the man and a cold chill ran down her spine. "No, wait, don't go." She looked up at Archie. "I think he's dead."

Archie knelt back down again. "Have you felt for his pulse?"

Eliza said nothing as Archie's fingers moved from the man's wrists to his neck before realisation crossed his face.

"You're right. He's gone."

Eliza jumped to her feet. "Oh my goodness, what do we do now?"

Archie shrugged. "I'll still have to go to the hospital and tell them to collect him, but I suppose it's less urgent now."

"It isn't less urgent!" Eliza's voice squeaked as she spoke. "You can't leave a dead body lying in the hallway. What if someone wants to visit?"

"I didn't mean it like that, you're right. We need to get him moved. I'll have to report it to the coroner while I'm at the hospital. Let me check if he's got anything on him that'll tell us who he is and where he's from."

"You mean touch him?"

"Of course touch him. You move out of the way and I'll do it."

Eliza stared at Archie as he rolled the body onto its back. "He said his name was Reginald White."

Archie felt the front of the man's coat. "Now, what's he got in his pockets?"

The outer pockets were empty of everything except a key and so Archie undid the buttons and reached into the inside pocket.

"What's this?" He pulled out a letter that Eliza took from him.

"It's addressed to a Mrs White, presumably his wife, and looks as if someone's already opened it." Eliza took the letter from the envelope and scanned it. "Oh my. Look at this.

To my darling H
How I long to be with you and make you my wife.
We've not much longer to wait, be patient, my love.
All will be well.
Forever yours
J

"Well, that's not a letter written by Mr White." Eliza forgot her squeamishness. "We need to find out who *J* is … and check whether *H* really is Mrs White."

Archie stood up and glared at her. "*We* don't have to do anything. I'll report the death to the coroner as soon as I get to work and he can get the police on the case. This isn't one of your newspaper stories, it's a real man lying in our hall."

Eliza's shoulders sagged. "I'm aware of that, but it might be tomorrow before the police arrive and we need to do something today. You need to make sure the post-mortem's held today as well. Judging by Mr White's symptoms, I'd say someone's poisoned him. If the body's left too long, all trace of it could disappear."

"That's enough, Eliza." Archie reached for the door handle. "Just get a sheet to cover the body and wait for me to come back. This is not something I want you getting involved with. Have I made myself clear?"

CHAPTER THREE

L eft alone in the hallway, Eliza put the letter into her pocket before setting off in search of Mrs Ellis. She found her at the kitchen table with Connie and the cook.

"Is everyone all right?" Eliza asked as she sat on the bench alongside Connie.

"They're both very shaken," Cook said. "They should lock up men like that, turning up at houses like this and frightening housekeepers half to death."

Eliza hesitated. "Yes, I suppose so, but the thing is ... he was rather ill."

Connie paused, her cup of tea halfway between the table and her lips. "Was?"

"Yes, I'm afraid so."

"Oh my goodness, it must be me!" Connie's cup crashed onto the saucer as she raised both hands to her cheeks. "Two men dead in two days."

"Don't be silly, of course it's not you," Eliza said. "He came to see Dr Thomson because he was ill and now we need to wait for a carriage to take him to the hospital. I want you all to stay in the kitchen until he's gone. Mrs Ellis, do you keep any sheets down here?"

"Sheets? You mean to cover the body?" Her eyes were wide.

"Don't worry about why I need them. Do you have any?"

"Only the best ones, but you can't use them. They'll be tainted."

Eliza nodded. "All right, where are the old ones?"

"They're on the top floor, near the guest room, but I can't go..."

"No, of course you can't. Let me do it." She stood up to leave. "Could you pour me some tea? I'll be back before it goes cold."

Eliza was halfway up the first flight of stairs when a voice called out behind her.

"Wait for me."

She turned to see Connie racing up the stairs after her. "What are you doing? Why didn't you wait downstairs?"

"I didn't want to stay with Mrs Ellis and Cook, they didn't seem comfortable with me there. I just won't look down the hallway."

"Come on then, let's hurry." Eliza shielded the body from Connie's view as they turned to go up the next flight of stairs. "Stop when you get to the second floor, I want to check something in Archie's study."

"Are you allowed in there?"

Eliza cocked her head to one side and grinned. "It's my house, I'll go in if I want to!"

Connie waited by the door to the study as Eliza walked in and began flicking her way through his bookcase.

"What are you looking for?"

"A book on drugs for the heart and anything he has on poisoning."

"Poisoning? You don't think…"

Eliza paused to study Connie. "Archie says I'm imagining it, but yes, I do. His behaviour, turning up here as he did, it wasn't normal."

"No, it was not!"

"Besides, the man said someone was trying to kill him. You can't ignore something like that. I need to convince Archie. Ah, here we are, this should tell me what I'm looking for." Eliza dropped a large textbook onto the desk and flipped it over to read the index.

"What *are* you looking for?"

"Atropine."

Connie shook her head. "Of course you are. Ask a silly question."

"It's a drug that's used to increase heart rate in people who have heart problems. They also use it to dilate the pupils."

"I'll take your word for it." Connie stepped into the room and sat in a chair beside the desk. "I still don't see what it's got to do with the man lying in the hallway."

"Mr White, of course. I need to get him covered up before Archie gets back." Eliza snapped the book shut and thrust it at Connie. "Here, take this to your room, I'll be back in a minute."

Eliza raced to the top floor and grabbed a sheet from the cupboard before hurrying back to the hall. She had no sooner covered the body when Archie walked in, leading two carriage drivers from the hospital.

"Here he is." Archie ignored Eliza as he pointed to the

body. "Can you take him to the morgue and I'll speak to the coroner later about a post-mortem?"

Eliza watched as the men wrapped Mr White in the sheet and carried him to the carriage.

"Didn't you speak to the coroner while you were at the hospital?" Eliza asked Archie once he returned to the house.

"No, I didn't, I was more concerned about getting the body out of our hallway."

"But the post-mortem's important. If someone poisoned him it needs to be done quickly before the drug disappears from his body."

"We don't know he was poisoned."

Eliza rolled her eyes. "Of course he was, didn't you see his face and eyes? If you ask me, I'd say it was belladonna, but if it is, the post-mortem won't find it unless it's done quickly."

Archie took her hands. "Stop worrying. I spoke to Dr Shaw while I was there and told him what had happened. He'll take care of it. I just need to fill in some forms first."

"Well, you need to be quick. I've found some books on atropine and belladonna poisoning and I'll read them while you fill in the forms. You will cite it as a possible cause of death on the form, won't you? It'll give them something to look for."

Archie sighed. "What did I tell you?"

"You need to include the letter and Mr White's statement that someone was trying to kill him as well. I read the letter again while you were out and I would say that Mr White was trying to tell us that his wife and her new love were trying to kill him. It all makes sense."

"It all makes sense if you're a journalist." Archie's brusque tone softened when he saw the look on Eliza's face. "All right.

I'll write a note to the coroner suggesting he may have been poisoned and take a copy of the letter. Will that keep you happy?"

Eliza smiled. "Yes, thank you. Let me go and get the letter. I was in Connie's room before you got home and left it up there. I'll bring it down to you."

Without another word, Eliza hurried up to the top floor before barging into Connie's room.

"Are you all right?" Connie asked as Eliza stood in the middle of the room, her eyes searching the shelves.

"Yes, I'm fine. I've persuaded Archie to take the letter to the coroner, but I need to copy it out before he does. Didn't I leave any writing paper in here for you?"

"Yes, it's in the drawer by the window, but why do you need a copy?"

Eliza paused and put her hands on her hips. "Because we're going to visit the address on the envelope this afternoon and I need to make a note of it."

"You can't turn up at someone's house, unannounced. Especially when you don't know them. What will you say?"

"I'm sure I'll think of something." With the writing paper in her hand, Eliza sat down at the desk to copy out the letter. "While you're waiting, can you find page three hundred and sixty-two in that book I gave you? I want to check my facts before we do anything else."

CHAPTER FOUR

The wind took Eliza's breath away as she and Connie stepped outside and she closed the door behind them.

Connie pulled her cloak more tightly around her. "Do you know where we're going?"

"Of course I do ... I asked Mrs Ellis when you went upstairs to fetch your cloak." Eliza grinned as she pointed to the left. "It's this way. Hold on to your hat."

The two of them put their heads down as they walked into the wind.

"Have you decided what you'll say?"

"No. It occurred to me over dinner that Mrs White might not even know her husband's dead. If Archie hasn't told the coroner, it won't have been passed to the police yet."

"Well, we can't do it." Connie stared at Eliza.

Eliza sighed. "We could go and ask after him, perhaps."

"We can't do that. What would she say if two strange women turned up on her doorstep asking after her husband?"

"Hmmm, you're right."

"Don't you think we should let the police deal with it like Dr Thomson said?"

Eliza ignored her friend. "If we just caught a glimpse of her, that might help. If she was in her mourning clothes, it wouldn't be so bad us turning up."

"What would you say?"

"I don't know, perhaps ask her if she knows anyone who might have wanted to kill her husband. Then I could pass the information to the police."

Connie giggled. "The police have got nothing to do with it; you're just nosey and like investigating murders."

Eliza grinned. "What's wrong with that? Don't you want to know who *H* and *J* are, not to mention what happened to Mr White? It's all very mysterious."

Fifteen minutes later they turned from the main road into a square flanked by two rows of large terraced houses.

"It's very smart around here," Connie said. "I can't imagine she'll answer her own front door."

"No, you're right. If this is where Mr White lived, he wasn't short of money. Now, we're looking for number forty-eight. It should be down here on the left." They counted down the numbers as they approached the middle of the street and stopped outside the house they were looking for.

"This is it." Eliza took a deep breath as she glanced around her. "I'll tell you what, there are some benches in the garden square, let's go and sit there while we decide what to say. I've been so busy concentrating on the road names, I need to compose myself."

They found a bench in a sheltered spot with a good view of the front door of number forty-eight. After a moment,

Eliza's brow creased. "What if *H* isn't Mr White's wife?" Perhaps she's the housekeeper ... or cook. Mrs White might be terribly upset."

A glint appeared in Connie's eyes. "Are you losing your nerve?"

"Not at all ... well, maybe a little. I've never done anything like this before. It's usually all set out in the newspaper for me."

"Well, you'd better make up your mind what you want to do, it's too cold to sit here."

Eliza nodded and pushed herself up but stopped and put a finger to her lips to silence Connie. "Look. A visitor."

A carriage, drawn by two immaculate brown horses, pulled up outside the house and Eliza and Connie moved towards the railings of the garden as an oversized, middle-aged man climbed out. He knocked on the front door of number forty-eight.

"I wonder who that is." Eliza watched as the housekeeper let him in.

"He certainly looked affluent with his top hat and tailcoat."

"Didn't he just." Eliza stepped back and studied the first-floor windows. "Look, he's up there ... with Mrs White, I presume. My, she's younger than I expected given Mr White's age, and very glamorous too."

"It looks like she's ready for a night on the town dressed like that," Connie said. "Look at that lace shawl she's wearing. That didn't come cheap."

"No, it didn't. Oh my goodness, look, he's kissing her!" Eliza's voice squeaked with excitement. "Do you think that's *J*?"

"I would say so."

The woman they presumed to be Mrs White smiled at the man before she disappeared from view.

"What are they doing now?" Connie said, as neither she nor Eliza took their eyes off the window.

"He looks quite happy with himself and so she can't have gone far. No, she's back, and she's giving him a drink. Champagne I'd say, judging by the glasses."

"Champagne!" Connie gasped. "At three o'clock in the afternoon!"

"Shhh ... don't make a noise." Eliza watched J make a toast.

"Do you think they're celebrating?" Connie's voice had returned to a whisper.

"I would say so, but would you really celebrate someone's death? It seems rather sinister."

"She might not know; she's not in her mourning clothes. What do we do now?"

Eliza put her hands to her face. "I don't know. We can't go and knock on the door while he's there, but we're only assuming this is Mrs H White and J. How do we find out for sure?"

"If you tell the police what we know, they'll be able to come and ask some questions. That would confirm it."

"Yes, you're right." Eliza's shoulders slumped.

"But you don't like that option?"

"No." Eliza pouted. "I wish we could do it ourselves and just tell them, but you're right. If that is J and he's more familiar with Mrs White than he should be, we can't just barge in ... especially not if he's celebrating killing a man. He might turn violent and Archie would kill me if we got into trouble."

Connie laughed. "He'd do no such thing, although I admit he wouldn't be happy. Let's get you home and you can decide what to do over a cup of tea."

CHAPTER FIVE

A s the afternoon drew to a close, Eliza handed Connie a glass of sherry and sat beside her on the settee.

"There's no point waiting for Archie, I've no idea what time he'll be home. He tells me when to expect him, but he's invariably late. If he isn't here in another ten minutes, we'll have dinner without him."

"Perhaps he's involved with the post-mortem," Connie said.

Eliza smiled. "You know how to cheer me up. I hope so, but if he is, he could be hours yet."

"Will you tell him we went to the house or will he be cross?"

"I'm sure he'll be cross, but I don't have much choice. The police need to know that the woman we think of as Mrs White is anything but a grieving widow."

"You said yourself, she might not know her husband's dead yet."

Eliza took a sip of her sherry. "Yes, you're right, I keep

forgetting that. Imagine if anything happened to Archie and I was walking around oblivious to the fact."

Connie stared down at her sherry before taking a large gulp. "It took them hours to tell me about Mr Appleton's accident when he had his fall."

"Oh, my dear, I'm so sorry." Eliza reached for Connie's free hand. "I didn't mean to upset you."

Connie glanced up, her eyes moist. "I know you didn't, I mentioned it because even though he didn't die immediately, I was so angry with the postmaster for not telling me sooner. It'd be scandalous if Mrs White hasn't been told by now."

"You're right, it would. I'm sure the hospital will have contacted the police."

Connie finished her sherry as Eliza stood up and offered her a hand. "Come on, let's get something to eat, we can't wait all night for Archie."

Eliza pulled on a bell cord before escorting Connie through the double doors into the dining room. "Take any seat, my dear. Mrs Ellis will be here in a moment."

"Wait for me," a voice boomed from the drawing room, and Eliza smiled as Archie strode through the door.

"You made it. We wondered if the post-mortem had delayed you."

"Um, no, not quite."

"Don't tell me it's not been done."

Archie looked visibly relieved as Mrs Ellis arrived and ladled soup into their bowls.

"Well?" Eliza said once they were alone again.

"We should do it tomorrow."

"What do you mean, *should*? Doesn't the coroner think it's urgent?"

Archie said nothing as he took a mouthful of soup.

"You haven't told him, have you?" Eliza said.

Archie put down his spoon. "It's not what it seems. I spoke to Dr Shaw first thing this morning, but by the time I got back to the hospital with the forms it was close to midday. He took them from me but said that after the shock of the morning, I needed to have a decent meal to perk me up."

"And so you went off for something to eat and did nothing about the body?"

"It wasn't like that. He came with me and paid for it. Not just in the hospital either, to a restaurant. He said that before he contacted the coroner he wanted me to tell him exactly what happened to make sure he had his facts right."

"And what did he say when you told him?"

"He was concerned, naturally, and said he'd write to the coroner immediately."

"A letter's no good, it will be too late by the time he gets it." Eliza felt the colour rising in her cheeks. "Why couldn't he go and see him this afternoon?"

"He was writing the letter this afternoon, as soon as we got back to the hospital. With the hospital mail being as fast as it is, the coroner should have received the details within the hour." Archie resumed his soup. "Dr Shaw left the hospital just before three o'clock and said he'd see me tomorrow. I had to do the ward round on my own, that's why I'm late."

Eliza took a deep breath followed by a mouthful of soup. A moment later she stopped and faced Archie. "Does that mean Mrs White doesn't know she's a widow yet?"

Archie's face paled. "I'm afraid so."

"My goodness, she'll be worried sick. She may be sitting at home waiting for him as we speak."

Archie held up his hands. "I'm sorry, you're right, the police need to be told. They'll only have the night officer on now and he won't do anything. How about I call at the police station first thing in the morning?"

"I suppose it's the best we can do at the moment."

Archie put a hand to his mouth. "I've just remembered, I gave the letter to Dr Shaw. We know nothing about the man except his name, it'll take them weeks to find him without an address."

Eliza rolled her eyes. "It's a good job you've got me then. I copied the address before you took the letter this morning. It was addressed to 48 Paulson Square."

"Did you memorise the contents of the letter as well?" The tone in Archie's voice wasn't complimentary.

Eliza grimaced at him. "I did better than that, I copied it out, not that you're taking it with you without me making another copy. That's how evidence gets lost."

Archie closed his eyes and lifted his face to the ceiling. "Evidence. Is that what this is all about?"

"At least one of us is taking this seriously." Eliza's spoon clanged on her bowl as she let it fall back into the soup. "Now promise me that first thing in the morning you'll go to the police station before calling on the coroner to make sure he got Dr Shaw's letter. You need to make sure they carry out the post-mortem without further delay."

Archie gritted his teeth. "Only if you promise to change the subject and let me eat in peace."

Eliza scowled before a smile flitted across her lips. "I will, but don't be fooled. I won't be so lenient tomorrow if nothing's been done."

CHAPTER SIX

I t was only half past seven the following morning when Eliza arrived for breakfast, but Archie was already there and about to finish his cup of tea.

"I've been thinking." Eliza slid into the chair alongside him. "You need to get to the hospital, I'll go to the police."

Archie glared at her. "You."

"Yes, why not? They do allow women into police stations. If you go, it'll take up too much time and getting the postmortem done today should be your priority. Don't forget, it's atropine you're looking for and it doesn't stay in the body long once it's been administered."

"Yes, I know all about it, thank you, but what about the police?"

"What about them? All I need to do is give them a few details of what happened and suggest they go and tell Mrs White the sad news about her husband."

Archie nodded. "I suppose so, as long as that's all you're up to."

Eliza feigned surprise, putting a hand to her chest. "Of course it is, what else would I do?"

"I never know with you." Archie gave her a sideways glance as he wiped his mouth on his napkin. "I'll see you this evening."

With Archie gone, Eliza hurried back upstairs and banged on Connie's door. "Are you awake yet?"

Connie was still in her nightdress as she opened the door. "I could hardly sleep with all that noise."

Eliza laughed. "I'm sorry. I wanted to tell you I'm taking an early breakfast and then going to the police station. If you want to come, you'd better be quick."

"I thought Dr Thomson was going."

"I didn't trust him to go to the police and the coroner and so I said I'd help out."

Connie raised an eyebrow. "And he said yes?"

"Why does everyone have such a poor impression of me? Of course he said yes. He said it made sense."

"Well in that case, give me five minutes and then ask Mrs Ellis if Cook can do me two soft-boiled eggs."

"They'll be ready and waiting." Eliza hurried back down the stairs stopping off in the study to grab a handful of paper. If this morning went to plan, she'd need something to make notes on.

An hour later, Eliza and Connie walked up the steps to the police station.

"Let me do the talking," Eliza said.

"I have every intention of, I've no idea what you're planning on saying."

"I'm going to report the murder." Eliza pushed through the large wooden door that opened into a small reception area. A desk sergeant glanced up as they walked in.

"Good morning, ladies." His greying moustache rippled as he smiled.

"Good morning, Sergeant. I do hope you can help us. My name's Mrs Thomson, wife of Dr Thomson from the Brompton Hospital, and this is my friend Mrs Appleton."

The sergeant nodded. "And I'm Sergeant Cox. What can I do for you?"

"Well, it's like this. We live in Halton Street and yesterday morning at about eight o'clock a man arrived at our front door and promptly collapsed in our hallway. He was looking for my husband in his medical capacity, but before he could be of any assistance, the man was dead."

"Dead?" the sergeant said.

"Yes, quite dead. The thing is, before he died he said there were people trying to murder him."

"Murder?" The sergeant's eyes were wide.

"Yes, precisely. Now, we know a few things about him. He told us his name was Reginald White, and he had a letter in his pocket addressed to a house on Paulson Square. My husband reported the incident to the hospital and the body's been taken there to await the coroner's inquest."

"The coroner?" The sergeant flicked through the large record book on the desk before him. "We've not had any instruction about a Mr White."

"No, I'm aware of that. Unfortunately, due to a delay at the hospital the formalities haven't been reported yet, but you see, that leaves us with a dilemma. I'm concerned that nobody's told the poor man's wife of her husband's demise."

"Yes, I see." The sergeant sucked air through his teeth as he wrote in his notepad.

"So will you do it?"

"Me?" The sergeant's eyes darted up to Eliza.

"Or one of your men?" Eliza smiled as she held his gaze.

"Well, I suppose somebody should ... but how do I know you're telling the truth without the coroner's report?"

"Because I'm not in the habit of visiting police stations to make up stories. Please, Sergeant, you have to trust me. There's a lady out there who doesn't know her husband's dead and she needs to be told. Imagine how you'd feel if your wife didn't come home and you didn't know where she was."

The sergeant shook his head, apparently lost for words as Eliza put the address she'd copied onto the counter.

"I've got this as well. There was an envelope in the man's pocket, which we passed to the coroner, but I copied the address from it. It's clearly addressed to his wife. That's how we know where she lives."

The sergeant stared at the paper. "There was no letter?"

"No." Eliza couldn't say why she didn't want to mention the note.

"Very well. I'll send someone as soon as I can."

"Thank you." Eliza paused. "When might that be? If it's not going to be too long, we'll sit and wait."

The sergeant's brow furrowed. "Wait?"

"Well, yes, so we can come with you. I'm sure Mrs White would appreciate some female company when the officer gives her the news. It might help her if she knows where Mr White was when he died. I can explain things to her." Eliza felt Connie's eyes boring into her. "I imagine it's difficult for a man to give a new widow such news."

The sergeant's cheeks reddened. "We don't usually involve members of the public in police work, especially not of this nature."

"I understand." Eliza gave the sergeant her best smile. "But is this case usual? And look at the address of the deceased. It's in quite a well-to-do part of town, I'm sure they'd like things done properly."

"Yes, I suppose so." The sergeant sighed. "Let me go and find someone to cover the desk and we can go together."

CHAPTER SEVEN

The sergeant knew the area well and twenty minutes later they arrived in Paulson Square.

"Number forty-eight's down here on the left." Eliza let the sergeant take the lead. "While we're here perhaps we could ask a few basic questions about Mr White to help the investigation along. There's no point visiting her more than necessary while she's in mourning."

The sergeant stared at her. "What sort of things?"

"Oh, you know, the usual." Eliza tried to sound casual. "Where did Mr White work, for example? They'll need to be told what's happened. Does she know why anyone would want him dead?"

The sergeant stopped. "We can't tell her he's been murdered. Until I hear the cause of death from the coroner we have to treat it as natural causes."

Eliza took a deep breath before she continued walking. "Very well."

The sergeant caught her up before instructing her and Connie to wait at the bottom of the steps. He knocked on the door and within seconds the housekeeper opened it causing Eliza to hurry to Sergeant Cox's side.

"Could we speak to Mrs White, please?" Sergeant Cox said.

"Have you seen the time?" The housekeeper crossed her arms in front of her. "It's not ten o'clock yet. You'll have to come back."

Sergeant Cox nodded before Eliza stepped across him, stopping him from leaving.

"I'm afraid that's out of the question," she said. "We've some rather urgent news for her. If you wouldn't mind telling her we're here, I'm sure she'll appreciate it."

The housekeeper eyed Eliza up and down before she turned back to Sergeant Cox. "I'll have to go and ask if she'll receive you. Who shall I say's calling?"

With the introductions complete, the maid closed the door leaving them on the doorstep.

"I don't suppose I'd let a group of strangers in without checking first," Connie said.

"We have a police officer with us, we're hardly likely to be up to no good."

"I suppose so. What will we do if she won't see us?"

"We won't take no for an answer, will we, Sergeant Cox?" Eliza glared at the sergeant who looked as if he'd rather not be there.

"We can't force our way in."

The housekeeper cut the sergeant's discomfort short when she arrived back and invited them up a flight of stairs into the drawing room.

"Mrs White will be down presently. She's most upset that you called so early but with the manners of the lady she is, she doesn't want to inconvenience you. She's even asked me to make you some tea."

"That's most kind, madam." Sergeant Cox inclined his head as she left the room.

"It's a very similar room to yours," Connie said to Eliza.

"Just bigger ... and they've removed the doors into the dining room." Eliza walked into the back room and peered out of the window. "They've a bigger garden too. I wonder if Mrs White will let me wander around it later."

"What on earth do you want to do that for?" Connie asked.

Eliza made sure the sergeant wasn't watching before she smirked at Connie. "No reason. I'd just like to see what she has down there." She wandered back into the drawing room as Mrs White arrived followed closely by a maid with a tea tray.

"Good morning, Sergeant." Mrs White extended her hand as if she expected him to kiss it but Sergeant Cox merely took hold of it and gave it a shake. "Please, take a seat. What can I do for you at this unearthly hour?"

"Well, madam." Sergeant Cox hesitated. "I wonder ... could you tell us when you last saw Mr White? This morning perhaps?"

If Mrs White was shocked by the question, she didn't show it. "My dear sergeant, my husband goes out to work in the middle of the night. How would you expect me to see him at a time my eyes are firmly shut?"

Sergeant Cox blushed. "I'm sorry, I had no idea. Perhaps last night, did you see him then?"

"As it happens I didn't. I was out at a cocktail party."

"But what about after the party ... you know, when..."

Mrs White laughed. "Are you trying to suggest I saw him

in bed, sergeant? Well, at the risk of embarrassing you, I must tell you that we have our own sleeping arrangements and so by the time I returned home I assumed he was in his own room."

"I see." The sergeant took a deep breath. "Could you tell us when you last saw him then?"

Mrs White paused. "Is today Thursday? Yes, of course it is. Well then, I didn't see him yesterday and probably not on Tuesday either; I was out that night too. It must have been Monday night."

"And you're not concerned about his well-being?" Eliza interrupted.

"Concerned? Why should I be?"

The sergeant coughed to clear his throat. "I'm afraid we've come with some bad news." He pointed to Eliza. "This is Mrs Thomson and she called to inform me that early yesterday morning a man we presume to be your husband arrived at her house, not far from here in fact, looking for a doctor. Mrs Thomson's husband is a doctor, but before he could help, the poor man was dead."

Mrs White stared at the sergeant. "What makes you think he was my husband?"

When Sergeant Cox struggled to find the words, Eliza spoke. "As he came into the house, he said his name was Reginald White. Was that your husband's name?"

Mrs White shuddered as her face paled. "How did you find out so quickly where he lived?"

"Unfortunately, once he'd passed away, we needed to check for anything that would confirm his identity and found an envelope with this address on. It was addressed to you."

Mrs White visibly flinched. "He had one of my letters?"

"No harm done." Sergeant Cox flashed Mrs White a broad smile. "There was no letter only the envelope. We just need you to confirm whether your husband's Christian name was Reginald."

Mrs White's eyes flicked to Eliza, who said nothing as she waited for a response.

"Yes, yes it was." Mrs White reached for her handkerchief. "Can you tell me why he died?"

"No, not yet," Eliza said. "My husband took him to the hospital and they expect the coroner to arrange for a post-mortem to find out."

"A post-mortem, oh my!" Mrs White buried her face in her hands. "My poor Reggie."

"We're so sorry," Eliza said. "This must be difficult for you. Do you have any children you could call on? It might help to be with someone else."

Mrs White shook her head. "We never..."

Eliza patted her hand. "I'm sorry. What about his employers then? Could you tell us where he worked? We'll need to tell them."

"At the bank." Mrs White's voice was barely audible as she spoke into her handkerchief.

"A bank? You said he left home in the middle of the night."

"Half past seven is the middle of the night as far as I'm concerned. How could we have a social life when he needed to be in work for eight o'clock each morning?"

Eliza rolled her eyes at Connie. "Can you tell us which bank he worked for?"

Mrs White paused for air. "Barclay and Company. He'd

been there for over ten years, although it was Goslings when he started."

Sergeant Cox took out his notepad. "Could you tell us which one? They have a number of branches."

"On Fleet Street."

The sergeant let out a low whistle. "That must have been quite a walk for him."

"Don't be ridiculous." Mrs White's tears suddenly vanished. "He took a carriage. He'd have had to leave at six o'clock if he walked."

"Yes, of course." Sergeant Cox lowered his head as he scribbled in his notepad.

"He must have had an impressive job, being there for so long," Eliza said.

"Hardly. He was a senior clerk."

Eliza glanced around at the expensive artwork on the walls.

"I have money in my own name," Mrs White said. "How else do you think we afford to live here? He only stayed at work to keep up appearances. He always worried that everyone thought he was a kept man."

"But it didn't bother you?"

"It bothered me that he would never escort me out of an evening. I was always the one who arrived at parties alone. How do you think that made me feel?"

"Terrible, I'm sure. Will you excuse me?" Connie stood up and marched to the door before turning to face Eliza. "I'll wait for you outside."

Eliza paused and stared at the door as it closed after Connie.

"I suppose we'd better go as well," Sergeant Cox said. "We've taken up enough of Mrs White's time as it is."

"We need to go?" Eliza glared at the sergeant. *How am I supposed to find out any more about Mr White?*

"Thank you, Sergeant. I'll call the housekeeper." Mrs White turned to ring a bell on the table beside her.

Eliza straightened her face. "I'm sorry we had to be the bearers of bad news, Mrs White. I'm sure you'll hear more from the coroner in due course."

Mrs White nodded as the housekeeper came to escort Eliza and the sergeant out. After a brief farewell, they headed for the stairs, but as they reached a half landing, Eliza stopped.

"What a lovely garden," she said to the housekeeper as she peered through the window. "Would you mind terribly if I took a quick look outside? I love gardens, but don't have much of one myself. Please."

The housekeeper sighed. "If you must, although I don't know what you expect to see. A plant's a plant if you ask me."

Eliza followed her through the kitchen and into the garden, indicating for the sergeant to follow her.

"Do you enjoy gardening, Sergeant?" Eliza asked.

"I have an allotment where I grow a few spuds and carrots. It gets me out the house."

"I always wanted a garden like this." Eliza glanced around at the shrubs that lined the edges of the flowerbeds. "It's lovely to see them all coming back into leaf after the winter. Look at the crocuses, don't you love their colours?"

"Will that do you?" The housekeeper shivered as she stood with her arms wrapped around herself.

Eliza did a final turn on the path that ran down the centre

of the lawn. She was about to head back to the house when she stopped and walked to the far side of the garden. "Just one more thing. Would you mind if I took a small cutting off this plant? I can't remember what it's called but it's an old favourite of mine and I don't have any at home."

"If you must." The housekeeper disappeared and returned a minute later with a pair of scissors. "Don't take too much."

Eliza found a shoot and cut it near the base. "There we are. Hopefully that will grow as big as this bush one day."

With the cutting in her handbag, Eliza and the sergeant walked back through the house and out onto the street. Connie was waiting for them on a bench in the gardens opposite.

"What have you been doing?" Connie asked. "I thought you'd follow me out."

"What possessed you to leave? I've never known you to do that before."

Connie's shoulders slumped as they started walking. "I'd had enough of her. We'd just told her that her husband was dead and she was more concerned about going to parties on her own. That was the last thing on my mind when they told me about Mr Appleton."

Eliza put a hand on Connie's shoulder. "Don't upset yourself. She's got her comeuppance now, she won't be going to any parties while she's in mourning."

"I don't imagine it'll stop her gentleman friend from calling though."

The sergeant's ears pricked up. "She has a gentleman friend?"

"She might have but we don't know for certain," Eliza

said. "Come along, we'd better be quick. We've got to get to the bank yet."

The sergeant stopped and stared at Eliza. "We're not going there now."

"But they need to be told why their senior clerk hasn't been in work for the last couple of days."

"Whether they do or not, it'll have to wait. Besides, this is police work. It was one thing taking you to Mrs White's, it's quite another to take you into a bank."

"But if you're not going to do it..."

"We will do it, but not now, and not with you. We have our procedures and I'm not treating it as a murder investigation until we hear from the coroner."

Eliza was about to argue but stopped and glanced at Connie. "Very well then. But can I leave it with you?"

"You may, and if your husband has an interest in the case I'm sure he'll be in touch with the coroner."

Sergeant Cox walked the ladies back to Halton Street, before he doubled back to return to the police station.

"I know that look, Eliza Thomson," Connie said, as the sergeant disappeared. "What are you up to?"

"If you were a bank manager and one of your staff didn't turn up for work, what would you do?"

Connie shrugged. "Probably nothing on the first day."

"But after that?"

"I don't know, look for him, I suppose."

"Exactly, but where would you start?"

Connie shrugged. "Why don't you just tell me?"

"Because I want to know if you're thinking the same as me. As far as the bank are concerned, Mr White's gone missing."

"He could be ill and hasn't told them. I doubt they suspect anything sinister."

"But if you were a senior clerk and had worked for the company for so long, wouldn't it be normal to send word to them? A telegram perhaps."

"I suppose so."

"And so when they didn't get any notification, don't you think they would've wondered where he was and perhaps reported him as a missing person?"

"To the police, you mean?"

A smile broke out across Eliza's face. "Exactly."

"But Sergeant Cox didn't know he was missing."

"No, but that's the point. Mr White worked on Fleet Street; we're in Chelsea. The bank wouldn't come here to report him missing; they'd report him locally. Come on, we're going to Fleet Street."

"We'll miss luncheon, more like," Connie said as Eliza hailed a carriage.

"Don't worry, we'll be there and back before it's served. I only want to ask the police a few questions."

CHAPTER EIGHT

With the midday traffic heavy, the carriage ride seemed to take an age.

"It's no wonder Mr White left home so early each morning if it took him this long to get here." Eliza leaned forward in her seat to peer through the window. "Now I know why Archie needed to move."

The horses stopped outside the police station and Eliza waited for the driver to help them down the carriage steps before heading for the door. A young man standing behind the desk glanced up and smiled as they entered.

"Good morning, Constable." Eliza returned his smile. "I'm here about a missing person and wondered if you could help."

"I'll try, can you give me the name?"

"Certainly, I'm here on behalf of a friend, Mrs White. It's her husband, you see, Mr White. He left for work two days ago and she hasn't seen him since. She's terribly worried."

The constable flicked to the most recent page of entries in one of the books before him.

"Now that's strange. You're the second person today to come in asking after him. It seems as if someone from the bank's reported him missing too."

Eliza put a hand to her mouth. "Oh my goodness, that doesn't sound good. Do you have any officers out looking for him?"

The constable shook his head. "Not at the moment. We've a couple of men not turned in this morning and we can't spare anyone at the moment. I expect we will as soon as we can." The constable continued reading. "Actually, no, I'll make sure the next man back goes straight out again. The note here says that Mr White recently took out life insurance for both him and his wife; the bank is worried someone may have found out. If anything's happened to Mr White, they fear Mrs White might be next. We need to find him."

"Oh my, Constable, you're frightening me now." Eliza's stomach churned as she gaped at Connie. "We need to go and tell Mrs White immediately and make sure she stays indoors. Thank goodness she has a staff to take care of her."

"Thank goodness, indeed," the constable said. "I'll make a note for a search of the local area to begin as soon as possible."

"Thank you so much, Constable, I do hope you find him. Now, we won't take up any more of your time, come along, Connie." With that she marched from the police station.

"What's the hurry?" Connie asked. "Are we going back to Mrs White's?"

"No ... not at the moment, anyway. I need a few minutes to think."

"Well, why didn't you tell the constable Mr White's already dead? They'll be wasting their time."

Eliza pursed her lips. "I thought about it but it would have spoiled the charade. We'll come back tomorrow and tell them. I don't suppose they'll spend much time looking today." They walked up to a waiting horse and carriage and Eliza gave the driver her address. "Come on, let's go home."

"Why aren't we going back to Mrs White's?" Connie asked as the carriage pulled away from the kerb. "You told the constable you were ... if her life's in danger, she ought to know."

"I know, but for some reason, I don't think she's in danger. Not yet, anyway."

"Why not?"

"Think about it. With Mr White dead who's the most likely person to get the life insurance money?"

Connie shrugged. "She is, I suppose. Unless perhaps he has a brother."

Eliza nodded. "That's an option but my guess is that the money will go to her."

"And so you think she's not in danger because she murdered Mr White to get the money and won't kill herself?"

"That's one explanation although I do wonder about the appearance of J, our mystery man."

"Of course, I'd forgotten about him. Perhaps he helped so he could settle down with a wealthy widow?"

"That's a possibility too, and it wouldn't surprise me if that's what happens. I fear that's not the end of it though."

"Why? What else could happen?"

"I don't know, maybe Archie's right and I do read too many murder stories, but when we saw J the other day, he looked like an affluent man already."

"He did, he wore a lovely suit and looked very smart."

Eliza leaned forward in her seat. "What if he has a taste

for expensive things but he's running out of money? Why not murder a man with life insurance and marry his widow. Then, all he'd need to do is make himself the beneficiary of her will and life insurance policy and take her life too."

"You mean he's a con man like the one we saw at the theatre the other evening?" Connie's eyes were wide. "Surely not. Can't a man marry a woman because he loves her?"

Eliza leaned back in the carriage and sighed. "I suppose he can, maybe I'm getting carried away. Don't mention that last bit to Archie, he'll think I'm stark, staring mad."

Connie's forehead wrinkled. "So, assuming that last thought is wrong, do you think J murdered Mr White so he could marry his wealthy widow, or was it Mrs White who did the killing so she could have the money and be with her new love?"

The carriage stopped outside Eliza's house and she sat forward in her seat. "It could be either. We really need to find out who J is. We can't draw any conclusions while he's such a mystery."

CHAPTER NINE

Connie stopped her crocheting and looked up as Eliza walked into the drawing room.

"I do apologise for being such a dreadful hostess this afternoon, my dear," Eliza said. "I got so carried away with those textbooks I didn't realise the time."

"I don't mind, I'm quite happy with my crocheting and Mrs Ellis has kept me supplied with tea. Did you find anything of interest?"

Eliza took a seat on the settee opposite Connie and helped herself to a cake. "I'm not sure. I need to speak to Archie. It's that cutting I took that's puzzling me. It's difficult to tell at this time of the year when the leaves are immature, but I'm sure it's belladonna."

Connie gave Eliza a blank stare.

"It's a poisonous plant," Eliza explained. "You've probably heard it called deadly nightshade."

"Oh yes, I've heard of that."

"Well, if it's eaten, it produces the symptoms we saw in Mr White. The trouble is, if you were going to kill someone with it you'd usually use the berries and obviously it doesn't have any at this time of the year."

"Maybe they were picked and dried ... or turned into jam? It's commonly done with other fruit."

"That's a thought." Eliza stared into space before grinning at Connie. "It's a good job you're here to remind me of all the domestic chores I never do. Whether the poison would survive the boiling or drying process though, I'm not sure. Another question for Archie."

"What else do you need to ask him?"

"Mainly whether he spoke to the coroner this morning and whether anyone did the post-mortem. I hope they did. I want his opinion on the cutting too, to see if he thinks it's belladonna. The books I've read say you can poison someone with the stems or roots, but it has a very bitter taste and so a person would notice before you gave them enough to kill them. I want to know what Archie knows about it."

Connie returned to her crocheting. "Hmmm, I'm afraid I can't help you there. I've never heard of anyone making jam out of roots, although I suppose all that sugar would help to mask the taste."

Eliza laughed. "It certainly would. Let me get another pot of tea and then Archie should be home."

Mrs Ellis was about to serve the dinner when Archie rushed into the dining room.

"I'm sorry I'm late, it's not been a good day."

Eliza let him take his seat and waited for Mrs Ellis to leave before she asked what had happened.

Archie grimaced. "I don't know where to start; at the beginning, I suppose. I spoke to the coroner first thing this morning, and it went downhill from there."

"Did he agree to the post-mortem being done today?"

Archie fidgeted with his soup spoon. "No, that was the thing. I was in his office by half past eight but Dr Shaw had beaten me to it. The coroner told me that they'd discussed the case and decided a post-mortem wasn't necessary."

Eliza spluttered on her soup. "Not necessary! How did they reach that conclusion about a man who turned up here with signs of poisoning and who died within minutes of telling us that someone was trying to kill him?"

"That's what I said, but the coroner told me that Dr Shaw was of the opinion we were making it up."

Eliza shook her head. "Why on earth would we do that?"

"I asked the exact same question and told the coroner exactly what had happened. He looked inclined to change his mind, but because of Dr Shaw's opposition to the post-mortem he said his department couldn't fund it. If I wanted a post-mortem doing, he said I'd have to do it myself."

"You! You haven't done one for years."

"I told him that too, but he said the only way he would agree to take the case was if I did it."

"So did you?" Eliza forgot about her soup as she gave Archie her full attention.

"What choice did I have? I took the body from the morgue and set it up in the lab, but then the most peculiar thing happened. Dr Shaw arrived. He was furious that I was doing the PM and told me to move to one side while he did it."

"So what did he find?"

"Well, that's the thing. Nothing. He dissected the main organs from the body and put them on a tray to take them through to the other room and then..." Archie put a hand to his head and stared at Eliza, as if afraid to speak.

"And then what?"

"And then ... he dropped the tray. It made such a noise that we both jumped and he stood on half the organs."

"He destroyed the evidence?"

"He said he hadn't, but I wasn't so sure. He collected them all up, ran them under the tap to get rid of the dirt and then did the tests on the washed tissue."

The blood drained from Eliza's face and she shook her head several times before she found any words. "Any traces of poison will have been lost. If poor Mr White was murdered, the killer's going to walk free."

When Archie didn't respond, Eliza looked over to see his face as white as hers felt.

"What haven't you told me?"

Archie took a deep breath. "I said a few things to Dr Shaw that I probably shouldn't have and we had quite a row. I stormed out of the office and went back to the morgue to see if I could salvage any tissue. The thing is, he followed me and accused me of tampering with the body to cover my tracks. He said he'd report me and suggest it was me who murdered Mr White."

For one of the few times in her life, Eliza was at a loss for words and she stared at her husband.

"Why would you have insisted on a post-mortem if you'd been the murderer?" Connie asked, filling the silence.

"Dr Shaw said I must have wanted to hide the evidence before they instructed anyone to do it."

Eliza recovered her senses. "He was the one who told the coroner the post-mortem wasn't necessary. If you hadn't said anything, nobody else would have looked at the body."

Archie's voice was quiet. "I told him that but he said he'd

had no such conversation and the post-mortem was booked in for later in the day."

"So the coroner lied?" Connie asked.

Archie nodded. "It would appear that one of them did."

Eliza stood up and paced the room. "Something's not right here and we need to find out what. They're not charging you with the murder of Mr White. Was Dr Shaw still at the hospital when you left?"

"No, he sent me off to do the ward round so he could write the report. When I got back, he'd disappeared."

"All right then. I suggest we take a carriage and go back to the hospital to find that report. It's too dark to get ours out and we can't wait until tomorrow, I won't sleep a wink tonight if we don't get this sorted out."

CHAPTER TEN

The sound of horses' hooves, not to mention wheels on gravel, was much louder than Eliza had ever noticed during the day, but the air was eerily silent at this time of night. The carriage pulled up alongside the right wing of the building as Eliza and Connie, covered with dark cloaks, followed Archie from the carriage.

"Don't do anything without me telling you," Archie said. "I'll be in trouble if anyone finds you here."

Eliza nodded but remained silent as they slipped through a side door before heading down to the basement.

"In here." Archie opened a heavy metal door and flicked on a dull lamp on the corner of a desk before ushering them inside. "This is Dr Shaw's office. He was writing the post-mortem report at his desk when he sent me onto the ward. Now, where is it? I want to see how he's going to explain away what happened earlier ... and check whether he makes any mention of me."

The desk was covered in papers but with little effort Archie found what he was looking for.

"Here we are."

Eliza moved to his side. "What does it say?" She scanned the first page as Archie read it. "Is that Dr Shaw's handwriting? It looks familiar."

"How can it be familiar, you don't know the man."

Eliza took the report from her husband and put it on the desk under the lamp. "I've definitely seen that writing before. Look at the extra twist on the Hs, I remember thinking it was unusual last time I saw it."

"Is it an H like the one in the letter?" Connie asked from the seat she'd taken in the corner. "That was distinctive."

"Yes, that's exactly it." Eliza's eyes shone as she smiled at her friend. "Whoever wrote this, wrote the letter to Mrs White." She turned to Archie. "What happened to the letter?"

Despite the dim light, Eliza saw the panic in Archie's eyes. "Dr Shaw took it from me. He said he'd passed it to the coroner."

"Did the coroner mention it when you saw him this morning?"

Archie shook his head. "No and I'd forgotten about it, so I didn't ask."

Eliza glanced around the room. "I'd say there's a good chance that letter's still here and we need to find it."

Eliza began searching the drawers on the left-hand side of the desk while Archie searched the right. Connie rifled through the bookcase. They worked in silence for several minutes before Eliza accidentally pulled the bottom drawer from its casing. The crash echoed around the room.

"What are you doing? Archie hissed.

"I'm sorry. There was something wedged at the back of

the drawer and I pulled harder than I needed to, to dislodge it." Kneeling down, she peered into the darkness beneath the remaining drawers and reached into the back. "Here we are, what's this?" She pushed herself to her feet. "The letter, look, I told you I'd seen that H before." She spread the letter on the desk alongside the report. "Don't tell me these documents were written by different people. They're identical."

"T-They can't be … it would be too much of a coincidence. Why would Mr White come looking for me of all people?"

"Maybe he deliberately sought you out." Eliza's eyes widened as she spoke. "When he arrived, he asked if you were the doctor. Maybe he came to you for a reason. It would explain Dr Shaw's bizarre behaviour over the post-mortem."

Archie took the letter from Eliza and studied. "J, I don't even know Dr Shaw's first name."

"Well, let's see if we can find it, shall we. There are enough papers on this desk, we should be able to find something." Archie watched in silence as Eliza and Connie started at the top and picked up one sheet of paper after another, checking for a name.

"He certainly liked a wager on the horses," Connie said. "There's a whole pile of betting slips here."

Eliza moved around to Connie's side of the desk. "Let me have a look." She studied the slips. "He's betting one or two pounds on each horse. Archie, did you know anything about this?"

"No, no idea."

"We need to find out if he ever won any money because his wages wouldn't last long if he didn't. If we can't find anything it might explain why he was so interested in a wealthy widow." Eliza's search grew more intense as she riffled through the papers finding nothing of interest until she reached the bottom of a large pile. "Oh, my goodness, what's this?" She pulled out a sheet of paper and stood up straight. "We've struck gold. A notice from a firm of debt collectors, addressed to Mr Joshua Shaw!" Eliza's eyes were wide as she stared from Connie to Archie. "We've found J!"

Archie's jaw dropped. "How could he."

"We need to get this to the police. Come on, let's go."

Archie remained by the desk as Eliza and Connie hurried to the door.

"We can't leave the desk like this, he'll know someone's been through his things."

"The man's a murderer!" Eliza failed to keep the exasperation from her voice. "He'll find out soon enough when the police get here."

"Quiet a minute, what's that noise?" Connie grabbed hold of Eliza's arm. "Someone's coming."

With a swift step backwards, Eliza pulled Connie into the wall as the door opened, shielding them from the man standing in the doorway.

"What's the meaning of this?" a voice boomed across the office as Archie stood frozen to the spot.

"I-I wondered ... I wondered if you'd written the post-mortem report. I wanted to read it."

"Without my permission?" The man moved towards the desk and Eliza put a hand over her mouth to suppress a squeal. It was the man from Mrs White's house.

"Were you about to tamper with the evidence ... again? I knew you were up to no good the moment you arrived here with that cock and bull story about a man turning up dead at your house."

"It's the truth, as well you know."

"I know nothing of the sort."

Connie's nails digging into her arm brought Eliza back to her senses. Her husband was facing a killer and she had to help him. Connie's face was white as she stood rooted to the spot but Eliza prised her fingers from her arm before indicating for her to move to the door. They had to get to the police station.

With a final glance at Archie, who had been backed into a corner on the far wall, Eliza grabbed Connie's hand and pulled her through the door. They crept down the corridor until they turned a corner to find the stairs. As soon as they cleared the last step, they broke into a run and didn't stop until they crashed through the doors of the police station where a startled Sergeant Cox jumped to his feet, his evening doze well and truly over.

CHAPTER ELEVEN

E liza and Connie stood with their hands on their hips as they gasped for air by the counter in the police station.

"What on earth's happened?" Sergeant Cox raised the counter of the desk and ushered them to the chairs opposite.

"Thank you, Sergeant, but we haven't got time to sit down. It's my husband, he's in terrible danger."

The sergeant took out his notepad and turned to an empty page. "You'd better tell me all about it."

"No, please, we really haven't got time. Can you get someone else to come with you and I'll explain on the way?"

Sergeant Cox hesitated before shouting through to the back room. "Jones, are you in there?" When he got no response he turned back to Eliza with a shrug of his shoulders. "I'm afraid I'm on my own. It's turned ten o'clock, you see, and we're usually quiet at this time. Jones must have been called out."

"While you were asleep," Eliza said.

"I wasn't asleep ... just thinking."

"Well, whatever you were doing, can you lock the doors

for an hour while you come and arrest our suspect? We know who murdered Mr White and he's currently alone with my husband. We don't want another death on our hands, do we?"

"No, of course not, but how can you be certain this man's the killer."

Eliza glared at the sergeant. "Please, lock the doors and walk with us and I'll tell you everything. We wouldn't have run the best part of half a mile if this wasn't urgent. We have to hurry."

Sergeant Cox winced under Eliza's glare and reached for a bunch of keys on a hook beside the door.

"All right, but you have to tell me what I'm walking into." He ushered them outside and turned the key in the lock.

"We've been able to identify the man we know as J, he's one of the senior doctors at the hospital."

"J?" The sergeant's forehead creased.

"The man who wrote the..." Eliza paused. "Oh ... we didn't tell you about that." She pursed her lips and took a deep breath. "I'm sorry, Sergeant. When we last called you we weren't entirely honest. You remember the envelope I mentioned with Mrs White's address on?"

"The one you said contained no letter?"

"Yes." Eliza grimaced. "Well, there was a letter. A love letter to Mrs White from a man called J. It was obvious it couldn't be from her husband, his name was Reginald, and so we suspected she had a new love in her life."

The sergeant shook his head. "A woman of her standing? That's outrageous. Poor Mr White. Are you suggesting he found the letter and they killed him because of it?"

"No, we're not suggesting that."

"It is an option though," Connie said.

"It is, but probably an unlikely one. Sergeant, after we left you earlier today, did you visit the bank as we discussed?"

"No, we didn't get around to it." The sergeant mumbled into his chest. "We were waiting for the coroner to contact us."

Eliza quickened her pace. "Well, it's a good job we did some investigating then. We found out from your colleagues near Fleet Street that Mr and Mrs White had recently taken out life insurance. We have reason to believe that the man we know as J had significant gambling debts and may have killed Mr White in order to marry his widow and get his hands on her money. There's even a chance that Mrs White could be next."

The sergeant wheezed as he tried to keep up with Eliza. "What's your husband got to do with this?"

"My husband works for J and he caught us in his office gathering evidence against him. When we left, he had my husband pinned against a wall."

"You've been breaking and entering? I could charge you for..."

Eliza's glare cut the sergeant off in mid-sentence. "I suggest you stop there, Sergeant. If you'd been more willing to investigate this yourselves, perhaps we wouldn't have had to."

The red-bricked facade of the hospital reared up out of the darkness as Eliza led them all around the corner. "Down here." She pointed to the side door that led to the basement. "And be quiet. We don't want him to know we're here."

The door to the office was still ajar when they arrived and a chill ran down Eliza's spine as she peered around it to see Archie in the middle of the room, a rope tying him to a chair.

She pushed on the door ready to march in but stopped when Dr Shaw spoke.

"I've no idea why that fool White came to your house on the morning he died, but unfortunately for you, he signed your death warrant."

"For God's sake, man, you can't go around killing everyone." Archie's voice had gone up an octave since Eliza had left. "When you became a doctor, you swore to reject harm and mischief, and yet what you're doing now is mischief of the highest order."

Eliza saw the perspiration rolling down the side of Archie's face, but Dr Shaw continued as if he hadn't spoken.

"I seem to remember you like a gin and tonic of an evening."

Eliza stared at the glass Dr Shaw held to Archie's lips.

"Mr White did too, and a good thing he did. The bitterness of the tonic..."

"No, stop." Eliza burst into the room and grabbed for the glass causing Dr Shaw to drop it into Archie's lap. "Sergeant Cox, arrest this man."

Dr Shaw took a step back as he studied the sergeant. "Good evening, Samuel. What are you doing here?"

Sergeant Cox looked from Eliza to the doctor. "Good evening Dr Shaw, Mrs Thomson invited me to join you. Can I ask what you were about to give Dr Thomson?"

"Just a taste of gin and tonic. Would you care for some?"

"It is not just gin and tonic." Eliza took the near empty glass from Archie's lap and glared at the doctor. "This needs to be analysed and when it is, I think you'll find it also contains extracts from the belladonna plant, or atropine to be precise. Isn't that right, Dr Shaw? You needed something bitter to mask the taste of the roots, but even tonic water wasn't quite bitter enough, was it? Mr White suspected that someone had poisoned him; that's why he came in search of my Archie."

The sound of his name jolted Archie from his trance. "That's right, Sergeant. Before you got here, Dr Shaw was boasting about how he'd prepared the poison from the plant in Mrs White's garden."

Eliza fumbled in her handbag before holding up the cutting she'd taken. "You mean this one."

Dr Shaw's eye's flicked to the door before they rested on the cutting in Eliza's hand.

Sergeant Cox reached out and pushed the door closed. "Don't think of escaping, Dr Shaw. We might be acquaintances, but I've seen enough here to arrest you for the murder of Mr White."

"B-But, it wasn't me. I didn't give him the drink. Hilda did."

"Hilda!" Eliza smiled at Connie as she put the cutting back in her bag. "So, H and J, Hilda and Joshua. You were in it together."

"No, it was her idea. I was only a companion for the parties she goes to."

Eliza's eyes turned to slits as she spoke to him. "But you wrote the letter telling her how much you wanted to make her your wife, and that you didn't have long to wait."

"It wasn't like that, she was the one who wanted to marry me, I only wrote it to keep her happy. I didn't mean it ... and I didn't poison her husband."

"I doubt Mrs White would have known she had deadly nightshade in her garden, or that you could use the roots to make a poison," Eliza said. "It would take someone with a medical background to realise that."

"No, you're wrong. She'd seen it in the newspaper. Someone else had used it to poison his wife and she asked me to help her. You have to believe me."

Connie cocked her head to one side. "If you're innocent, why were you trying to poison Dr Thomson? Did you want to keep her company on the gallows?"

"No..." Dr Shaw's eyes flashed around the room. "I wouldn't have done it. I only wanted to scare him."

Eliza stepped to Archie's side and undid the knot in the rope. "And would you have scared Mrs White into paying off all your gambling debts as well?"

"She has enough money. She wouldn't have missed it."

Sergeant Cox stepped forward and took hold of Dr Shaw's arm. "That's enough, sir. I'm arresting you for being an accomplice to the murder of Mr White. Mrs White will also be charged."

Dr Shaw pushed the sergeant against the wall before heading for the door, but Archie caught his free hand.

"Oh no you don't, you're not going anywhere, Dr Shaw. Sergeant, do you have your handcuffs?"

Sergeant Cox regained his balance and forced Dr Shaw to the wall before turning him around and securing his hands. "That'll do it. Shall we go? We need to get him behind bars before we pay Mrs White a visit."

Connie followed the sergeant but Archie waited while Eliza stopped to collect up the glass and a selection of papers from the desk.

"We need to get the liquid in this glass analysed. Shall we take it back to the police station as evidence?"

"We can't do that," Archie said. "We'll take it to the lab before we go so they can analyse it. If we leave it lying around some other poor soul may take a fancy to it and we can't take any chances."

Eliza nodded. "You're right, they can take a look at this cutting for me while they're at it."

CHAPTER TWELVE

A young constable sat at the desk as they walked into the police station and he leapt to his feet when Sergeant Cox marched in.

"Sergeant, what's going on? I only slipped outside for five minutes and when I came back..."

"Save the excuses, laddie." The sergeant pushed Dr Shaw towards the cell at the back of the police station. "Bring the keys to the cell and make sure Dr Shaw here doesn't cause any trouble."

"Has he been up to no good?" The constable smirked as Sergeant Cox pushed the doctor into the cell.

"You could say that, now lock the door and make sure you keep the key in the desk. I have to go out again, but should be back within the hour with another prisoner."

"Another one! We've had no one in the cells for months and now we have two in one night. Are you going to tell me what happened?"

"You'll hear soon enough, but not now, we're in a hurry.

Do not open that cell under any circumstances, do you hear me?"

With an assurance from the constable they could trust him, Sergeant Cox ushered Eliza, Connie and Archie back outside.

"Back to Paulson Street then."

Archie held out his arm for Eliza to link. "You seem to know an awful lot about what's been happening. You haven't been getting in the sergeant's way, I hope."

Eliza's eyes narrowed. "Of course not, but it's a good job I do know what's happened otherwise you might have gone the same way as Mr White."

Archie paled. "Don't remind me. Do you really think he had belladonna in that tonic water?"

Eliza squeezed Archie's arm. "It wouldn't surprise me. It's as good a way as any to get the poison into someone, wouldn't you say?"

"I suppose so, but where did you find that cutting?"

Sergeant Cox chuckled. "She told a good old tale to get us into Mrs White's garden. Even had me fooled to start with."

Archie did a double take. "You've been in Mrs White's garden with Sergeant Cox? Just stop one moment, you need to tell me what you've been up to."

Eliza stroked his hand and smiled. "And we will, once we have Mrs White locked up. Come along, we're nearly there."

It took several attempts of hammering on the door before the housekeeper came to answer it.

"Have you any idea what time it is?" She'd clearly been in bed and only pulled the door as wide as the chain allowed.

"Can we come in, madam? We have an urgent need to speak to Mrs White."

Eliza had never heard Sergeant Cox sound so officious.

"I imagine she'll be in bed by now. Can you come back in the morning?"

Sergeant Cox pulled his truncheon from the pouch on his belt. "I'm afraid not, madam, and if you don't let us in, I'll have to use force."

The housekeeper let out a squeal before she stared at each person on the doorstep.

"I can't let the men in, I'm not decent."

Archie took off his coat and offered it to her. "Madam, I'm a doctor of medicine and have seen many a woman in her nightgown. If it makes you feel more comfortable, please slip this on. We have no time to lose."

Slowly, the maid closed the door enough to remove the chain and then took Archie's coat before she let them in. "I'll take you upstairs."

Knocking on Mrs White's bedroom door, the housekeeper asked them all to stand back while she opened the door an inch. She lowered her voice to speak.

"Mrs White, are you awake?"

When there was no answer, she pushed the door slightly further ajar. "Mrs White, the policeman's here to see you again."

When there was again no answer, Sergeant Cox stepped towards the door and banged on it with his truncheon.

"Mrs White. This is Sergeant Cox. I need to speak to you as a matter of urgency. If you don't come to the door by the count of three, I'll have no choice but to come in. One, two ... I'm coming in one more count. Three."

Sergeant Cox pushed past the housekeeper to find himself standing in an empty room. "She's not here."

"Of course she's here... "The housekeeper joined him and stared at the bed that had been turned down sometime earlier.

"What was that noise?" Connie rushed back to the stairs. "She's down there. Quick."

Sergeant Cox took the stairs two at a time and caught up with Mrs White as she reached the hallway. "Are you going somewhere, madam?"

"I was on my way out, I didn't realise I had guests."

"You're going out!" Connie couldn't hide the disgust in her voice. "You only found out you were a widow yesterday, you should be in mourning."

Sergeant Cox grabbed Mrs White's arm. "You're not going anywhere. Mrs White, I'm arresting you for the murder of your husband."

Eliza hurried down the stairs but as she approached the bottom there was a thud and she glanced up to see Mrs White in a heap on the hall floor.

"Leave her where she is." Archie overtook Eliza and knelt by Mrs White's side before opening the neck of her blouse. "She's fainted. Does anyone have any smelling salts?"

The housekeeper rushed down to the kitchen and returned with them a moment later.

By the time Archie held them under her nose, Mrs White was already regaining consciousness but he continued anyway to make sure she was fully alert.

The housekeeper pushed past Eliza to tend to her mistress. "Bring her up to the drawing room, she'll be more comfortable there."

While Mrs White was being helped upstairs by Archie and Sergeant Cox, Eliza slipped into the kitchen to get the bottle of tonic that had been on a shelf earlier that day.

"Can I assume that neither you nor Cook drink tonic water?" Eliza asked the housekeeper who followed her into the room.

The housekeeper shuddered. "Dreadful stuff. A waste of good gin pouring that stuff onto it. Cook can't understand the attraction either."

"It's fortunate you don't. Shall we go?"

By the time Eliza arrived in the drawing room, Mrs White was sitting in a chair by the still glowing fire while Archie poured her a glass of brandy.

"As soon as you've had that, we need you down at the station," Sergeant Cox said.

"But I haven't done anything. Why would I kill my Reggie?"

"Perhaps because he had recently taken out life insurance for the two of you," Eliza said. "It appears you enjoy the finer things in life but I spotted a number of final demands for payment in the kitchen. Was your money running out and you thought the insurance would help you out?"

"No, it wasn't like that. I didn't want to hurt Reggie, he was a dear man, but..." Mrs White stopped and she buried her face in her handkerchief.

"But what?" Sergeant Cooper asked.

When Mrs White failed to answer, Eliza responded. "It wasn't your idea, was it, Mrs White?"

Mrs White shook her head as her sobs became louder.

"Did Dr Shaw make you do it?"

Instantly, the sobbing stopped and Mrs White stared at Eliza. "How did you know?"

Eliza sat on the chair next to Mrs White. "We weren't strictly truthful with you earlier. The envelope we told you about did contain a letter, from someone called J to yourself. We found out after we left here that J is Dr Shaw. Was he your new love?"

"No! How can you say that? We're friends and I enjoy his company. He often accompanied me to parties when Reggie was too tired."

"So why did you ask him to help you murder Mr White?"

"I didn't!" Mrs White's voice squeaked as tears returned to her eyes. "It was his idea. I foolishly mentioned that Reggie had got us both life insurance policies, and he came up with the idea. He wanted the money and when I tried to stop him he became angry."

"You seemed quite happy together yesterday afternoon when we saw you through the window. You looked like you were drinking champagne and toasting a special occasion."

Archie's mouth dropped open as he listened to Eliza.

"That was his idea, he brought the champagne with him."

"Because he'd heard your husband was dead?"

Mrs White rubbed her hands across her face. "I have a plant in the garden he told me was poisonous. I had no idea, but he saw it and said that if he prepared the poison, all I had to do was pour Reggie a drink."

"And the poison was in this bottle?" Eliza held up the tonic she had placed on the sideboard.

"Yes." Mrs White began crying again. "He told me I had to use it to make Reggie a gin and tonic each evening for a week, but not to drink any myself. I was too frightened to argue. He's a big man, and I worried he'd hurt me if I didn't do what he said."

"Had he spoken of marrying you once you were a widow?" Eliza asked.

"Yes, that was his plan. He said he wanted to take care of me and that we'd be married as soon as I was out of mourning."

"Did you want to marry him?"

Mrs White blew her nose and took a gulp of brandy. "I don't know. Perhaps. I did like him but I didn't want Reggie to die. Please, you have to believe me."

"Did Mr White notice the tonic tasted different?" Archie asked.

"No, I don't think so. At first it didn't seem to have any effect, but after about four days I became frightened. Reggie would tell me he was seeing things and on the morning he died he said there were snakes climbing the walls."

"You told us you hadn't seen him that morning," Eliza said.

"I was frightened you'd think I had something to do with his death." Mrs White finished her brandy. "But I sent him to a doctor. I wanted him to get well again."

"You sent him?" Archie said. "How did you know about me?"

"You?" Mrs White studied Archie as if she was seeing him for the first time.

"I'm Dr Thomson. Your husband came to our house yesterday morning asking for me."

It was as if a veil had been lifted from Mrs White's eyes. "So that's why you're here. I didn't realise I'd sent Reggie to you specifically, I'd just heard Dr Shaw talk about a doctor who lived locally."

"What had he said?" Eliza's eyes narrowed as she spoke.

Mrs White placed the back of a hand on her forehead. "Oh, I don't remember the details, only that one of the doctors who worked for him lived nearby and he mentioned your address. For some reason I remembered it and when Reggie became ill, I panicked and told him to go and find you."

Archie stared at Eliza and then back at Mrs White.

"Dr Shaw wanted me to take the blame for this all along. After all I've done for him and this is how he thanks me."

Sergeant Cox used the pause in the conversation to walk towards Mrs White. "Madam, whether or not you meant to kill your husband, I believe you delivered the fatal dose of deadly nightshade. You need to come with me to the police station. I'm charging you with the manslaughter of Mr White. It will be up to the judge to decide whether it's you or Dr Shaw who's telling the truth."

CHAPTER THIRTEEN

It was almost ten o'clock the following morning when Eliza arrived in the dining room to find Connie waiting for her.

"I heard you pottering around in your bedroom and so I told Mrs Ellis we'd have breakfast together at ten," Connie said.

"That's very thoughtful. After what happened yesterday I couldn't sleep, everything was racing through my head. To think, Archie could have been murdered!" She put a hand to her chest as Connie poured her a cup of tea.

"Well, thanks to you, he wasn't. I presume he's gone to work?"

"I imagine so. I must have dropped off around seven and when I woke up he'd gone. Poor thing. I don't think he slept much either. Still, I'm hoping that now Dr Shaw's behind bars, Archie may get his job. He'll be the most senior doctor in the department and he's been more than patient. If he can get a senior physician role, Father might take him more seriously."

"Well, at least some good may come from it then."

As the clocks struck ten o'clock, Mrs Ellis arrived with a

tray bearing softly boiled eggs, toast and a fresh pot of tea. "Will that be all, madam?"

"Yes, thank you. I'll ring if we need anything else."

Mrs Ellis had no sooner disappeared than the dining room door opened and Archie joined them. Eliza couldn't fail to notice the red rims around his eyes and his dishevelled hair.

"What are you doing here? I thought you'd be at work."

Archie sat down and reached for a slice of toast. "I can't work after everything that happened yesterday. I popped into the hospital and told one of the juniors to check on the patients, I needed to go to the police station."

"Was Sergeant Cox still there?"

"He was, poor fellow. He looked exhausted but had to wait for an inspector from New Scotland Yard to arrive."

"Did he get anything more out of Dr Shaw or Mrs White after we left?"

Archie smiled. "He did. Once we'd gone, they had a huge row though the bars of the cells. Sergeant Cox listened in, of course, and finally Dr Shaw conceded it was all his idea. He said he wouldn't have hurt Mrs White if she'd refused to co-operate, but did admit to blackmailing her."

"Blackmail?"

"Apparently he'd threatened to tell her social circle about their friendship and suggest it was more intimate than it was."

"Well, she fooled us," Connie said as she took the top off an egg.

Eliza laughed. "She did, it looked very intimate from where we were standing."

Archie frowned. "Yes, I need to ask you where you were standing but perhaps not now. Anyway, she said their relationship was purely functional and that he was nothing

74

more than an escort. If her friends thought otherwise, she'd die of shame and so she did what he told her."

"So, will she still be charged?"

Archie nodded. "Probably, but with a lesser charge. He'll be charged with murder, of course, and will probably hang."

Eliza shook her head. "All because of his gambling debts. What a foolish man. Still, look on the bright side. You must be in with a good chance of getting his job once the hospital board hear what's happened."

Archie shook his head. "I don't want it."

"You don't want it? Why on earth not, after all these years?"

Archie sat back in his chair and shrugged. "Dr Shaw had planned everything so I took the blame. He thought I was about to get his job and admitted to Sergeant Cox that he deliberately gave Mrs White my address so they would find the body here. He also bribed the coroner to avoid a formal post-mortem, so I'd have to do it instead. Once he was sure I'd taken the bait he deliberately sabotaged it to destroy the evidence and my reputation."

"But that's no reason not to apply for his position."

"It is." Archie rubbed a hand across his unshaven chin. "People talk and in a hospital like ours it won't be long before everyone knows what happened. They won't talk about the fact I was innocent, it will be all finger-pointing and talk of how Dr Shaw manipulated me."

"But that's nonsense."

"Maybe, but that's how it is. I can't stay there any more. Once I've had a cup of tea I'm going to the hospital to hand in my notice."

Eliza stared at him. "You can't leave without getting a

position somewhere else. What will we do for money? And how will we be able to keep this house? We can't keep going back to Father."

Archie sighed. "I'll find something. There are plenty of other hospitals in London."

"But you'll end up in a junior role again, when you should be one of the most senior doctors in London."

Archie said nothing as he flicked crumbs around his plate.

"Can I make a suggestion?" Connie's face flushed as both Eliza and Archie stared at her. "It's none of my business but, if you remember, Dr Jacobs from the surgery in Moreton-on-Thames died earlier this week. They'll be looking for someone to replace him ... perhaps you could become the village doctor?" Connie shifted in her seat when she got no response. "Oh well, it was only a thought."

"And it was a good thought." Eliza took Archie's hand. "What do you say? You'd be your own boss then."

Archie glanced around the elaborately decorated dining room. "We've only just moved here, we can't move again. Besides, I don't know whether I'm cut out to be a village doctor, doing everything myself."

"You needn't do everything yourself, I can help you." Eliza squeezed his hand. "Why don't we at least visit Moreton? You've never been and I'm sure you'd love it."

Archie eyed the two women. "All right. I'm not promising anything, but ask Mrs Ellis for another pot of tea and I'll think about it."

THANK YOU FOR READING!

I hope you enjoyed the book. If you did, I'd be grateful if you could leave a review.

As well as making me happy, reviews help the book gain visibility and bring it to the attention of readers who may enjoy it.

To leave a review, visit your local Amazon store and find my author page by typing VL McBeath into the search bar.

Once there, click on *A Deadly Tonic*, scroll down to the review section and click on "Write a Customer Review".

My only plea. Please no spoilers!

*

If you'd like to keep in touch with further books and special offers in the series, join my newsletter here:

https://www.subscribepage.com/ETI_SignUp

Thank You!

AUTHOR'S NOTE

After working on my historical family saga series for the last 7 years, moving into cozy mysteries has been something of a change. I've always loved the works of *Agatha Christie* and similar authors and I hope I've captured some of their essence in this series.

Eliza was inspired by one of my characters in The *Ambition & Destiny* Series - Harriet. She was a fabulous character to write about but had a very difficult life. This was in contrast to her sister-in-law, Charlotte, who had the (mostly) constant support of her father, Mr Wetherby.

This led me to think 'What if Harriet had enjoyed a more charmed life?' 'What if she'd had the same opportunities as Charlotte?' and 'What if she'd had a father like Mr Wetherby - only nicer?'

That was how Eliza was 'born'.

I hope you'll join me as she moves to Moreton-on-Thames and settles into her new life ... with a mix of murder and mystery thrown in for good measure!

ACKNOWLEDGMENTS

As ever when writing a book, I couldn't have done it alone.

I would like to give special thanks to my friend Rachel, my husband Stuart, and dad Terry for reviewing all the books in the series so far and providing much appreciated feedback.

I would also like to thank my editor Susan Cunningham and cover designer Michelle Abrahall for helping me make the books look, and read, as professional as possible.

The series is certainly better for everyone's input.

Thank you!

ALSO BY VL MCBEATH

Eliza Thomson Investigates

Murder in Moreton

Death of an Honourable Gent

Dying for a Garden Party

Look out for the newsletter that will include details of launch dates and special offers.

To sign up visit: https://www.subscribepage.com/ETI_SignUp

~

The *Ambition & Destiny* Series

Based on a true story of one family's trials, tribulations and triumphs as they seek their fortune in Victorian-era England.

Short Story Prequel: *Condemned by Fate*

(available as a FREE download when you buy Part 1)

Part 1: *Hooks & Eyes*

Part 2: *Less Than Equals*

Part 3: *When Time Runs Out*

Part 4: *Only One Winner*

Part 5: *Different World*

For further details, visit VL McBeath's Amazon Author Page

Made in the USA
San Bernardino, CA
04 November 2019

59385023R00056